7 On The Back

Adrian McKenzie

All words and cover design © Adrian McKenzie 2020
Not to be replicated without permission

Dedicated to those who pushed me out of my comfort zone and helped my light to shine.

Contents

- I Wanna Hear Poetry
- Tea & Toast
- With or Without
- How to stay in The Friend Zone
- Dear Caramel
- Anansi
- L1
- Wembley at The Oval
- Jumble Sale Chic
- Crystal Eyes
- Dovedale
- Mama Says
- Road Worthy
- Cerulean Gold Rush
- Scream
- Doorsteps to Heaven
- Meerkat
- In Public / In Private

In the beginning there was "Ztylez" (styles)
And Ztylez begat Poetic7
And Poetic7 begat Adrian

I Wanna Hear Poetry

I wanna hear rivers of exceeding beauty
I wanna see the soundtrack to your silent movie
I want to feel the earth shake without me moving
I wanna see bravado displayed demurely

I wanna be the lead character in your cast of extras
The last piece of toast you eat for breakfast
Your by-the-book driver behaving reckless
I wanna know your combination of verbs and adjectives

I wanna see your face for radio in high definition
Walk under a ladder to test your superstition
I wanna know how many ways you go fishing
I wanna see if you can handle a hardcore rhythm

I wanna hear a word that's on point and educating
I want a Power Point Presentation - without the powerpoint presentation
I want intonation, inspiration and entertainment
I want to hear … animation

I wanna hear the same thing as your millionth viewer on you tube
I wanna hear old words on a new tune
I wanna hear poetry
I wanna hear poetry
I wanna hear you

Tea & Toast

Rambling Rambo's ransacked revered rustics
Memories are now marked by crowdfunded eulogies
Noodles jack knife with forks in the road so...
Screw your normal, slowly

Saunter solemnly when told to
Know you, trust memes and grow
Gallantly ghost cos loyalty's corny
Trust me, screw your normal

You suit your ties,
Skies are beneath us
Steam rises so boil up all your ingredients
Screw Your Normal, feel good

With or Without

Cop a cup of copper comfort
Hunger's where things crumble
For better or worse what to do first?
Cause of death office grumbles?

Leaves or bags, white or black
Milk, sugar, leave the spoon in
Off the boil or hot to trot
Burnt tongues aren't the coolest

Who wants to look foolish?

Karen wants it Karen white, add a K for good measure
Dude at the back wants it strong and black, Spike Lee should make him an extra
78 degrees and their special teas should be lined up as well...
Don't forget the plate of biccies, do you want to go to hell?

Dip em, dunk em, or munch em, crunchy
Those are words of war
Drink coffee instead, a wise one said
Or read the list on the staff room door

How to stay in the Friend Zone

You've got a style that most mamas trash
Your make up makes my soul wake up but it ain't MAC lads
I don't care about the size of your saddle bags
You're that type of cat lady that doesn't have cat
The type
Always busy editing your habitat
Is your name Cat Kidston
As a matter of fact don't answer that
You'll make a Christian Bale from the Woolworth tower brewing Teasdale until Yorkshire screams appropriation
Joker
I'm the mocha brown bird in the lighted window striving to ignite what might make your spine tingle
Yet if death is kind I'll breathe your white honeysuckle for more than a single hour in starlight
I wanna play dot to dot with your plot holes until your middle fingers are invites to examine your light from every angle say from sunset to sunrise
You're embedded in my mind like a journalist behind the line of fire singing burn baby burn
See I've been admiring you with these red birds since 6am and at 1.35 I'm wondering if this amateur drivel goes with your clothes.
You're a smouldering porcelain anarchistic Portman, a frosted rose

Anything from your cherry lips could make the sun feel cold
That smile that makes my mirror crack.
This poem is the love child of Pavlovs dog and Schrodingers cat
Forget perfect 7's, I want 69 eyes to testify that we're bad like blue-nosed policies but well-read with real power.
I don't believe in binary scales cos if we're 1 then our silent battles will be two.
Maybe this just selfishness or a sentiment that's well over due.
Maybe this is just Maslow from 5 to 3 to you.
I don't know so...
Peace out 86 from yours the 82.

Dear Caramel

Dear Caramel

You gave me sensual touches like feather blushes
My insides were scrumptious like a summer time bee buzzing
I be like birds buzzing
Because bees are busy hustling honey makers
We spin acres like the planet of love orbiting Canaan
Our connection was the promised-land
Relaxed like agape hands
Isn't yours the promised hand?
Thoughts played me as the one man banned from your heart and that's painful
We were engaging like alliteration
You were the pigment that coloured my imagination
I was word play and you were quotation
Food for thought and every time I said grace
I saw you

Dear Caramel

In your ground I grew
Till I became the tree whose groves you knew
We made sounds and grooved
Danced all the moves
In my heart
Our duet was in tune
We had pleasurable text

When we made love, love
Our energies were too bright to reflect
Moon River would bend the light
But the bulb was from the straight vine
And the blossoming situation would fruitfully delight

Dear Caramel

Every time I close my eyes I photosynthesize
Frame your melody and burn with desires
Twirl you like spires
Climb your inner mountains
Drink of your fountains and light fires
Your words fuel me to fly higher
Inspire
Never run flat because you're my battery and tires
Together we'll survive on this rocky road

Dear Caramel
You're the caramel inside my chocolate soul
You're the cream that ices me and completes the cake
I just hope you know this and feel the same way

Anansi

A Yo
Mi name Anansi I
Rasta four eye
Actually 10 eye
Mi nuh business if yuh want fi dead I
Mi a cotch like so
An me a cotch like so
Skin teeth and mek yu cry
Put on yuh slippers
Yuh can't catch I
Try fi whack I an' me a go dutty yuh carpet
Middle of the night a when yuh go work di hardest
Unno tink seh mi nasty but rass yuh a try fi lick me
Right
Wi mi dying breath me go sen' fi mi pickney

L1

I don't know if we lost them
Can we find them if where they went, they don't want to be found?
Are they inspiring, or just, not around.
Is their energy hardwired into every person that said nice things?
What if my life while they lived didn't make them proud?
What changes now?
Who gives who the how to, live like the first thing we say every time it ends for someone else?
For a few days, maybe a month in the next six or 12 then it's whatever happens on earth stays there and somehow the sign language of death can't fall on deaf ears.
We yield to the same old diet unless required.
Why can't we believe they're gone when we believe that...
They're still here, so we say.
Reincarnated in hearts, arts, preserved in photo frames.
Nothing new from them today or tomorrow.
Their news will be old news until the cycle consumes you.
Have you already counted the cost of being a loss?
Are you burying treasure to be found later?
You'll never hear what they say when your day comes

Wembley at The Oval

Before rain stops play
Take the ball and spin it past your posts.
Past keepers of old scores and goals
Past makers of mounds and moulds
Bounce it so hard they duck and you break yours

Guardian angels, serendipitous saviours
Field favours like spring weddings
Take the ball and spread it in every direction
Passing jams like your sat nav
Greased palms don't always make for great catches

Run after what matters
Shedding blocks at every line of scrimmage
Your circle's centre doesn't have to have you in it

See worlds and be water until the land is in view
Eat trigger stew if you've the appetite to handle it
Applaud other's pressured passages
Play percentages for averages even when yours is banterous

Know that when you're engaged, momentary marriages are manageable, momentous and magnanimous

Old Spice can't always create classics and our links might die in battle but if we're on the field then maybe ours is the day

So what will you do before the rain stops play?

Jumble Sale Chic

Where is the beauty?
When you decide that that pair of shoes with coloured laces is in fashion?
When you see them every day on your way to work and play.
You know they're not just for a sunny day in June but you hide them away
When wearing them you'd be another somebody that the majority may pass by.
Your laces and heel trim sparkle to squeeze compliments that are really condiments.
Ponder this, would you be full if they were the meal and be able to live if they stopped?
Yet still you keep this pair of shoes in a box.

Where is the beauty?
When that top from the sale that fits your shape sits waiting for the right light.
You say you bought it in the autumn for all seasons.
You wanted to unleash it ahead of the New Year, new me brigade.
Yet it hangs there with the tags on sighing, lamenting the sight of the others.
Among many colours its truth remains scarlet while your readiness fades.
When you finally wear it do you expect to hear the words stunning...and brave?

If my glass is half full maybe I can't see the fight.
In this motorcade of emotes, votes and likes it would be helpful if you could take a no make-up selfie sometime
Post it offline where I can see you better.
Print it, sign it, pronounce your name phonetically, and rewrite it alphabetically.
Wear that sweater and shoes if the combination is right.
In this age of click and swipe are you even your type?
Where is the beauty when you don't know that?
I'm happy to help you find it

Dismissive demeanours leave us blinded and so private we screen time.
Before we let anyone else use ours we rewind and ensure they know that the bridge is drawn.
We squeeze grapes for wine and olives for their oil
Not every Garden of Eden is in need of a stone wall
Wear those shoes, wear them all and put comfort to the test

Where is the beauty if the truth is suppressed?

Crystal Eyes

Is your past a foreign country?
If so how often do you visit?
Is it for business or for pleasure ?
Is it secluded or touristic?
Do you have a holiday home or no go areas within it?
Does it have monumental cities?
Are your memories memorials or are they living exhibits?
If I'd like to go there...what's the cost of ticket?
Could I go for a moment?
Would I be there in a minute?
Is it a place of worship, do others go there on pilgrimage?
As a travel destination what star rating would you give it?

If your past was a pack of cards, would you be willing to deal it?
Is it a feted piece of literature that limits your life's vocabulary.
Is it a path that panders to extinction?
Do you marry your past to your present in tensions?
Is your past the blessing you were cursed with?
Is it the margin of error that makes you live second to second?
Is your past a day of lessons that you're simply letting slide

Is your past a persistent researcher that you're simply walking by?
Is your past the death of you or what makes you feel alive
Is your past a foreign country?

Dovedale

Amidst the clapping trees and booming hills
She stood

Frozen like taxes until her interest rate rose
Trying to catch the note of the strumming stream

As the whispering wind started rumours
She believed
She'd fall
Pregnant with fear
Her comfort zone was born

Bairns skipping over stepping stones
Each step changing tones
By this river I have known
She stood

Humming the note of the strumming stream
Thawing out thoughts of why

This filly affiliated with feeling afraid
Her feelings were frayed yet
She walked over water like cobbled stones were her disciples

Stepping out like her faith says
Converting the unbeliever inside her
Drowned in joy, I was
We sang the song of stepping stones in harmony
For amidst the clapping trees, above the roaring hills
She soared

Mama Says

We laughed at their masks.
Their strain revealed our faces.
Now they sip tea from flasks.
Mama said every 10 years there are changes.

We laughed at watching others being watched
Proclaimed our freedoms were the greatest.
Black pots and kettles are being washed.
Mama knows the road we're taking

We lapped up their graft with contactless lusts.
Our canned candid's are on binary shelves.
Black spots with white heads are tasked squeezing
with trust from thrust.
Mama sandbags her brood from incoming hell

We laughed at their cooing for independence
Bolted doors with keys covered in their sweat
Welcomed them back with cracked cups of help me.
Mama said the devil knows who to use when under
threat.

We lapped up our luxuries like locusts
On cue we were wholesome aliens
Had showdowns over plastic roses because we never
voted to sew them.
Mama said do you see what I've been saying?

Mama believes - mama steps.
Mama sees - mama says.
Mama gleans - mama preps.

Mama needs - mama gets.
Mama reads - mama protects.
Mama reveals - mama accepts

We will linger in laughter lost to gargled gallons of gloom.
The strain of estrangement replaced by kisses on unsaved faces.
We will find fingers of fumbling pharaohs humbly gloved by nature's broom.
We hope.

Road Worthy

Empty roads like outgrown clothes
Ignored moans, untold stories on dog-eared notes
Scrunched up and thrown
Only unrolled at deaths, marriages or birth
Empty roads that once knew their worth
Now un-changed underwear with stains of the after birth
Is charity what these roads deserve?
Though coasts coax lazy fire makers, nobody dares to strike them.
Ignite them
Why are children frightened of the night time dark in their home but not the clouds?
Many won't swim with the tides of change afraid to drown

Empty roads chock with 2nd hand clothes
Where many met at the clock
Now after 5.30 everything is closed
The Tam-o-Shanter's old
Tea rooms and coffee shops worn
Who wants to live here?
Or who'll admit that they do.
Ayr
Blue as Caucasian veins or the flag
Where the fish and chips and ice cream ain't bad
It's a couple of drams away from the bottle.

A place between the edge of flattened earthly hopes
and a base for better orbits
Maybe empty roads are better as launch pads
Note pads
Napkins to wipe bloodied mouths
Maybe who they want, is unavailable, to retrace them
Draw them towards a better place on the map.
For now it's a case of wear the gastro hat
If it wasn't for locals would they be known to the crowd?
Empty roads
A home, for now.

Cerulean Gold Rush

Developing shades of Rubik's hues rearrange me daily
I'm just grateful that, I've got hand sanitiser
bubblegum flavoured
If I taste it, will my words be cleaner?
Will the contactless swipes of open mouthed smiles place me in danger.
Will dirty scoundrels panic by me in the Tesco queue?
These the bubbles upon which I chew.
I breathe
I smell blue
Fresh as skies without planes and cars.
The only see side I know now a face on a screen from a far.
I smell blue.
Sinking sorrows over solemn stories from six degrees of separation.
Sweetness soured by selfish sods.
I chew on what remains and gums our times.
I smell the chance to truly sanitise.

Scream

I dare you to scream
Be loud
Be less than proud
Scream the house down
Throw your voice around
Bounce off the walls like Aladdin's genie
Scream reams of rage until nobody wants to play your stage
Scream so revealing they can't accuse you of script stealing
Your story is your story so awards and book glory for being gory is the last thing you need
Scream until you can afford to put trauma in storage or set opening and closing times for those memory banks
Some only scream when the world can see them.
What help do they need if the blood on their hands is in stride with their climb through the ranks?
Scream until you find new notes in your glands
Scream to pull the sun through the clouds.
Scream to bring heaven down
Scream if you've passed exams or are sick of being passed on
Scream if you feel you can't master pasta
Scream if you don't want your pain plastered from Maastricht to Perth
Scream if your highest height is your nose above dirt

Scream if you finally know your worth and you're alive
in a time when you can't find any hurt
Scream if being last feels like being first.
Scream if you want to burst but you can't because
you're mopping up for someone else
Scream because it's good for your health
Scream because you need to fight the infection.
Use every inflection
I dare you to scream because you require direction.
Make a scene to find a place in yours
Scream yourself hoarse
Scream to avert wars
You can be a banshee or like nails on a chalkboard

Once you know who and what you're screaming for
do it with all your might
You might just save a life.
Keep Screaming.

Doorsteps to Heaven

We clapped
    Like wind up monkeys with plastic drums
    For the unsung,
    For those risking their life biting their tongue
    Along with those who'd say leave them in the slums
    Along with those who are amassing sums while we dwindle to none

And we clapped
    Tears streaming like Netflix marathons
    Hearts touched by everything but hands
    Housing estates became rivers of Babylon
    For 5 minutes in the evening we were at one
    We remembered Albion

And we clapped
    Alliances masked like the news buried in mass graves of live love laugh
    Our fuel prices falling
    Curtain twitching diagnosed as exercise
    Was it the state's mind?
    Be kind or be labelled
    See you next Thursday

And we clapped
>   With the face of a goose fat smothered potato
>   We who took our rage to Facebook
>   We who took our rage to the papers
>   We who took our rage to radio

And we clapped
>   As house of entertainment became morgues
>   Zooming on a graveside the norm
>   Not knowing if our neighbours are timing our runs and walks
>   Hoping hope is buying a new set clothes
>   Believing the most beautiful flowers will grow

And we clapped
>   Honouring heroes without hazmats
>   Finding favour for the feeble that we ignored weeks ago
>   Believing hugs are for the thugs not social contracts
>   Knowing the only accounts held to are the one's overdrawn
>   Getting to know mute, block and unfriend a lot more
>   New day, new laws, new world new norms

And we clapped
    Until our hands were sore from holding up our end of the bargain
    Using life hacks to journal the uncertain
    Knowing that kindness has to be a way of life to be a virtue
    Wanting to know weren't alone, hurting

And we clapped
And we clapped
And we clapped

Twilight

Hold me high above the water away from the cabal of the clouds
I am grounded by governing growls
Mounds mill around the face of my path
Space is my front ear so I listen for the wafts of change
I am arraigned by the season and seem to suffer in silence
Hold me high above the water ways of the violent, the wicked,
Some say float the boat or we won't stick with it
Buttress anchors with the canon of kisses or well-known scripts
What's worth when your face won't fit?
Can't you hide me away until it's my time to tick?
Every page in my chapter is ripped, giving me so many paper cuts I'm losing my grip

Boxes of broken promises seduce dust in open plan offices
Blue sky theology breaks saints into sinners
Mosh pits of expiring potential sold to the highest grinner
Fed up to be vegan to be a chicken dinner, hold me
Hold me high above the high ways and moral grounds
Whose really above see level? My math can't figure it out.

Misery hounds nibble on my very nuggets of gold
Bound like a slave to a system on which I remain unsold.
If I decide to come out I'm panned for being so bold.
Will the rainbow catch me if I'm 50 shades of grey?
I guess you'll have to hide me away

Barricade me behind brushed chrome benevolence, drapes
Feed me with the darling buds of May as you play all my songs on masking tapes
Salty is what the weathermen say when they speak my name.
I am peaky, blinded by glimpses of humans using in sense to purge the earth.
The better we match, the more I burn so hold me
Hold me down so I can hold you up
Hide me away where moth and rust cannot corrupt
If love is the glue why do we live unstuck?
We won't know if we're hiding away.

Meerkat

My poetry does not come with public vulnerability insurance
The sort that hides me away if I breakdown on stage.
The spotlight doesn't spot the difference between my highs and lows or rights and wrongs.
I can't backspace or control alter and delete when I falter.
If I freeze I've got to wait until this radio head tunes into the right frequency and says OK computer.
I eye moments when my cap turns backwards and my relationships don't feel dated.
I hate this, cling film wrapped cling film that I call poetry of the fingernails
I bite anything just to get a grip, I want a taste of that rocket ship.
Dig deep to get a lift until the soil needs fertility treatment.
What's weakness? A car without fuel
Every time I compare the market for a quote, I'm told I'm not premium.
Always adding features that are rarely needed or desired
Bred well but that yeast infection has ceased the rise.
Damn I rhymed in couplets, I've been trying not to do it.
I should be the human cat video or at least use crass humour

See this poetry doesn't come with public liability insurance.
The type that prevents you from hearing anything untoward, opinionated or unrehearsed.
If it's not drowned in the gravy it's not worth being on stages because silence is death
Yet the policy that says I must be confined to race, love and childhood, resemble the rest is all in my head.
Supposedly I'm supposed to be read, that's what real poets are like aren't they?
Real poets write about local things, ice creams, van themes, daisy chains and Viking dreams.
I should be rhyming what's viral on repeat, not a widescreen live stream of shootings in the street.
Not another cracker whacking Huey Newton off beat, there's only room for three and they're all on TV or ethnic radio.
This poetry will never come with a, hey mum, I've made it so, I guess I'll need home insurance.
The type that says you're home when you're sure that you believe what you say.
The type that contains terms that others care to translate if you speak their language.
The type with the clause that grips everyone who arrives to listen.
The type that highlights lowlights without venom via familiar incisions.
Speak to the soul but Blanche your face or catch a case of inciting division

Be the tall type that has the cladding that Grenfell didn't
I'm done speaking with rhythm, it's too black, too stereotypical
Should I bathe in muddy puddles just to grab colour to ink with or
Does this poetry need insurance?

In Public / In Private

In Public
I Am

Softly spoken
A razor
Random flavours
Reserved until acclimated
Low maintenance
Impossibly Patient
A buffet breaker
Perfectly parked after a thousand manoeuvres
Watch the car!
Snake hipped groover
One of you lot
No hoo hah
A Fence sitter
Opinion splitter
Small eyed cos the heart is bigger
Straight laced
Gracious but gated
Tidy
Scrub up stylish
Cheese nemesis
Freestyler
Coriander is the devil
Reluctant first mover
All about the music
Purposeful passion producer

What's black got to with it?
Food critic
Subway shareholder
Indecisive as to whether KFC or Nandos are my Greggs
All legs
Seeking worlds without a passport
Wondering what I need a mask for and wearing it anyway
Anyway

In private
I Am

A fugitive from the bay of pirates
A Black Panther before you said Wakanda
Blood type Pedantic
Statement towels and mugs
A Speech Thug and Grammar Nazi
Accent attempter
Head renter
Short tempered
Spender
Amazon wishlist for 5 years and wonder why it's not in stock type
Good nights sober
Say OK a lot
Body conscious
Mama's boy

Consumate cancerian
Huggable
Contrarian
Mayonnaise librarian
Gin carer
Rum King pin
Diving champion in the king sized bed division
Sellotape wizard
Bare feet and shorts around the house in winter
Sometime singer
House heated to Jamaica
Mental mountain rescue
Bless You and thanks
Yankee Candles
Lush lover
Niche chugger
Rabbit hole dweller
Crate digger
Cushions and curtains
Poignant Present giver
Dry as Australian sandpaper
Sports gamer
Ball breaker
Bull crap contact tracer
Hand grenades and hot sauce
Word Play and metaphors

Hi my name is Adrian
Have we met before?

Printed in Great Britain
by Amazon